GO, MO, GO!

MONSTER MOUNTAIN CHASE

Mo Farah

Hodder
Children's
Books

Little Mo and his **four best friends** had just come back from a long cross-country run.

"How many countries did we cross?" panted Lily.

"Four," said Mo.

"I loved the view from the top of the Eiffel Tower!" said Vern.

1

"It was **really hot** at the top of those pyramids!" gasped Banjo. "And **really chilly** at the top of Mount Everest!" shivered Lily. "And **very muddy** along

the Amazon river!"

laughed Lyra.

"Good fun though,"

said Mo. "France, Egypt, Tibet and Brazil

all in one go. Now that's what I call a

cross-country run!"

"I'm hungry," said Vern.

"I'm thirsty," said Lyra.

"Me too," said Mo, draining the last drop from his water bottle. "I think the next time we go running we should take two bottles of water and some sandwiches too. Especially if we're running a really long way."

The five friends sat in a circle on the grass and began to untie their shoelaces.

"Where shall we run tomorrow then?" said Lily, starting to get her breath back.

"Somewhere we've never run before," said Banjo.

"Somewhere beautiful," said Lyra.

"Somewhere breath-taking," said Vern.

"Somewhere with lots of bushes in case we need a wee," said Banjo.

"How about somewhere that's really beautiful, wild and free, with sunshine and shade, with green fields and blue skies, with wild flowers and tall trees, forest tracks and winding ridges with glistening snow at the top and sparkling lakes at the bottom, plus waterfalls to send our Pooh sticks down too?"

"Sounds perfect!" grinned Lyra.

"Then the Rocky Mountains it is!" said Mo, springing to his feet. "We'll run the entire length of the Rocky Mountains, from Canada all the way down to the bottom of North America."

"Wow!" said Banjo. "Sounds brilliant! I've always wanted to visit the

Rocky Mountains. I've seen them on the telly but I bet they look amazing right up close!"

"I bet the Rocky Mountains are **immense!**" said Vern.

"I bet the Rocky Mountains are **awesome!**" said Lily.

"I bet the **Rocky Mountains rock!**" laughed Banjo.

"There's only one way to find out," smiled Mo, draping his trainers over his shoulders and turning in the direction of home. "See you tomorrow, bright and early," he said with a wave. "And **don't forget your sandwiches!**"

At sunrise the next morning, the five

friends gathered together again and started to limber up. **Limbering-up exercises are really important** if you are going to go for a long run. Especially if you are running around the world.

"Has everyone remembered their sandwiches?" asked Mo, raising his knees to his chin.

"Sure have!" said Vern, squatting low and then jumping into the air. "I've put mine in my rucksack."

"Me too!" said Lyra, tightening her shoulder straps and then bending down to touch her toes.

"Sandwiches packed!" said Lily and

Banjo, jogging on the spot.

"Then as soon as we've finished warming up, we'll get going," said Mo.

The five friends had five exercises to do before setting off on their run. Each one was specially designed to warm up their muscles and get their legs stretched and ready for running.

"How long is the Rocky Mountain range?" asked Vern.

"It stretches more than **three thousand miles**, across seven states from British Columbia all the way down to New Mexico," said Mo. "There are **five mountains** in the range, and the **tallest one is over four**

thousand, four hundred metres high!" He grinned.

"Sounds like you've done your homework!" said Banjo, striding low and twisting his body left and then right. **"I always do my homework before a run!"** smiled Mo. "The more you know about the route you're taking, the fewer surprises there'll be!"

"I'll be surprised if there aren't a few surprises along the way today," said Banjo. "There seem to be surprises around every corner when we go on our runs." **"Those zombie camels** that chased us round the pyramids

yesterday were a bit of a surprise!" said
Lyra.

"And **that yeti** that chased us all
the way down to the bottom of Mount
Everest was a bit of a **surprise
too!**" nodded Lily.

"Yes, where did he come from?!" asked

Banjo. **"I thought he was a big hairy snowball until I saw his teeth!"**

"Thank goodness for avalanches," said Lily. "If there hadn't been an avalanche we'd never have got to the bottom of Everest as fast as we did."

"And that yeti wouldn't have been buried under the snow!" said Vern.

"Along with my bobble hat," frowned Banjo. "I loved that bobble hat – my auntie knitted it for me. I wonder who's wearing it now?"

"Well, hopefully there won't be any surprises today," said Mo. **"And if there are, all we**

have to do is **RUN!**"

"We're good at running!" smiled Lily.

"We certainly are," said Vern. "No mountain is too high!"

"No valley is too low!" said Lily.

"No distance is too far!" said Lyra.

"How far away are the Rocky Mountains?" asked Banjo, sitting on the grass and hugging his shins.

"About six thousand, seven hundred

kilometres," said Mo, doing a high kick.

"Wow!" said Lily. "This really is going to be a long run!"

"Sure is!" said Mo. "And the sooner we get started, the better!"

With their limbering-up exercises completed, their water bottles full and their sandwiches packed, the five friends exchanged fist-bumps and then lined up ready to go.

"On our marks," said Lyra . . .

"Get set!" smiled Banjo . . .

"Get really set . . ." grinned Lily . . .

"Get really really set . . ." laughed Vern . . .

"GO!" shouted Mo.

They were off!

By the time the five friends reached the Canadian State of British Columbia **they didn't just need a drink, they needed a lie-down too.**

"It's everything you said it would be!" gasped Vern, lying on his back on a carpet of wild flowers and gazing up at the snow-topped peaks of the Rocky Mountains. **"The sky is so blue!"** panted Lyra, pulling her water bottle from her rucksack and raising it to her lips. **"The grass is so green, the trees are so tall!"**

Vern and Lyra were right. The mountain valley that stretched before them was truly a sight to behold.

"I wish I'd brought my dog," said Banjo, picking up a stick and hurling it as far as he could across the flower-filled meadow. "He'd love to be here with us now, fetching sticks!"

"I wish I'd brought my budgie," said Lily,

prising open the stopper on her own water bottle. "I wish she could hear those birds singing. I've never heard tweets like them." **"Listen to the bees too,"** smiled Banjo. **"Have you ever heard buzzes that loud before?!"**

"Run!" shouted

Mo, jumping to his feet and ramming his water bottle back into his rucksack.

Lily, Lyra, Banjo and Vern sat up and looked round in astonishment.

"Why are we running?"

they asked, snatching gulps from their water bottles and then racing to catch up with Mo.

"They're not bees, they're wasps!" said Mo, motioning behind him. "The stick Banjo just threw **landed on a wasp nest!**"

Banjo, Lyra, Lily and Vern looked over their shoulders. Mo was right.

A cloud of angry wasps had erupted from a hole below ground and was swarming straight towards them.

"There's thousands of them!" shrieked Vern, leaping over a fallen tree.

"Looks like millions to me!" squeaked Banjo.

"Sounds like zillions to me!" squealed Lyra.

"**RUN** like you've never run before!" shouted

Mo at the top of his voice. "And don't stop till we get to Alberta!"

By the time the five friends reached the State of Alberta they didn't just need a drink and a lie-down, they needed something to eat too.

"Anyone fancy a sandwich?" panted Lyra, removing her rucksack from her shoulders.

"Have the wasps gone?" panted Vern, hiding behind the trunk of a tree and hardly daring to peep round.

"I can't see any," gasped Lily.

"I can't hear any," wheezed Banjo.

"The wasps have gone," smiled Mo. "And a sandwich is a very good idea!"

"I think we deserve some grub after

running this far!" smiled Lyra, greedily yanking her home-made sandwiches from the bottom of her rucksack, and prising open the silver foil.

"Run!" cried Mo,

jumping to his feet before Lyra had even had a chance to take a bite!

Lyra sprang to her feet, sandwich in hand.

"Why are we running?"

she gasped.

"GRIZZLY BEARS!" shouted Mo. "We're being chased by Rocky Mountain grizzly bears!!!!!"

Lyra, Lily, Banjo and Vern glanced over their shoulders.

Mo was right. Hundreds of grizzly bears were bounding down the valley sides and heading straight towards them!

"What have you got in your sandwiches?"

shouted Mo, hurdling a

Rocky Mountain stream.

"HONEY!"

shouted Lyra.

"Bears love honey," gulped Banjo.

"Bears adore honey!" shuddered Vern.

"That's why they're chasing us!" shouted Mo. **"They like honey sandwiches just as much as Lyra does!"**

"What am I going to do?" gasped Lyra, tightening her grip on her sandwiches as she hurdled another stream.

"Throw your sandwiches over your shoulder and RUN as fast as you can!" shouted Mo.

Lyra plucked her sandwiches from their silver foil, and hurled them into the air. **"I've done it!"** she shouted. **"NOW KEEP RUNNING!"** shouted Mo. **"And don't stop till we get to Idaho!"**

By the time the five friends reached the American State of Idaho they didn't just need a drink, a lie-down and something to eat, they needed twenty minutes of total silence to get their breath back.

"Sandwich?" said Vern, breaking the silence, prising the lid from his sandwich box and generously offering to share.

"Run!" shouted Mo, jumping to his feet before Vern had even had a chance to take a sandwich out of the box.

Vern jumped up like a jack-in-the-box and clutched his sandwich box to his chest.

"Why are we running?" he gasped.

"WOLVES!" shouted Mo. **"We're being circled by Rocky Mountain wolves!"**

Shivers ran down the backs of the five friends as the **blood-curdling howls** of a hungry wolf pack echoed through the valley.

"What have you got in your sandwiches?" shouted Mo, zigzagging through a maze of rocks and bushes.

"Lamb with mint sauce!" shouted Vern.

"Wolves love lamb with mint sauce!" shouted Banjo.

"Especially the lamb bit!!!" shrieked Lyra, batting a low-hanging tree branch from her face and racing after her four friends.

"Throw your sandwiches over your shoulder like Lyra did," shouted Lily, "or we'll end up as sandwiches too!"

35

Vern glanced anxiously down at his sandwich box, prised open the lid and then jettisoned his beloved sandwiches over his shoulder.

"Sandwiches away!!!" he shouted.

"Good!" shouted Mo. **"Now everyone keep running and don't stop till we get to Montana!"**

By the time the five friends reached the State of Montana they didn't just need a drink, a lie-down, something to eat and twenty minutes of total silence to get their breath back. They needed a place to cool down fast, too.

"This way!" shouted Mo, pointing to the top of a distant waterfall.

"We're not going to climb right up there, are we?" gulped Lily, raising her eyes to the craggy mountain skyline and counting each slippery rock as she went.

"No," laughed Mo, **"we're going to cool down in the pool at the bottom!"**

"We can fill up our water bottles too!" smiled Lyra, fanning her face with a fern leaf.

"Are you sure the wolves have gone?" asked Vern, peering inside his sandwich box and finding not so much as a crumb.

"The wolves have long gone," smiled Mo, bounding away across the rocks with an empty water bottle in each hand. **"We can relax now!"** His voice echoed.

Mo was right. The tranquil pool at the bottom of the waterfall was the perfect place to cool down and rest.

"I needed that!" spluttered

Banjo, raising his head from below river level and shaking his wet hair like a dog.

"Me too," said Lily, plunging both hands into the crystal-clear water and dabbing her face with it.

"Is anybody hungry?" smiled Mo, pulling the rucksack from his back. "That sawn-off tree trunk will make a perfect dining table."

"I'm starving," said Vern.

"I could eat a horse," said Lily.

"I could eat an elephant!" said Lyra.

"I could eat a herd of elephants!" laughed Banjo,

brushing the top of the sawn-off trunk with his hand and sitting down cross-legged on the grass.

"Room for four more?" smiled Lily, kneeling alongside him and then beckoning the others to follow.

It was heaven. The sun was shining, the water was glittering and for the first time since arriving in the Rocky Mountains, the chance of a proper picnic loomed.

"Sandwich, anybody?" said Lily,

"Yes, sandwich, anybody?" said Mo.

"What you have you got in yours?" asked Lily, kneeling

down beside Mo and unzipping the seal on her sandwich bag.

"Salmon," said Mo. **"There's lots of protein in salmon!"**

"I've got turkey in mine," said, Lily, unwrapping the silver foil carefully and giving her sandwiches a sniff. **"There's lots of turkey in turkey!"** she laughed.

"I've got cheese and pickle in mine," said Banjo, unclipping the lid of his lunch box. "If we put all our sandwiches out in the middle of the tree trunk we can have a proper **Rocky Mountain feast!**"

"RUN!" cried Mo,

suddenly
jumping to his feet
and pointing at
the sky.

"RUN!" said Lyra, springing to her feet too and pointing at the mountain ridge.

"RUN!" shrieked Vern, and pointed to the forest floor.

"FISH EAGLES!"
"MOUNTAIN LIONS!"
"WOLVERINES!"

Picnic time was over. One sniff of sandwiches and a squadron of fish eagles had filled the sky, a pride of mountain lions had lined the rocky ridge and an army of wolverines had come charging out of the forest.

"Fish eagles love salmon!" hollered Mo.

"Mountain lions love turkey!!" shrieked Lily, leaping up from the grass.

"I guess wolverines must love cheese and pickle!!!" squeaked Banjo, trying to uncross his legs as fast as he could.

"What's a wolverine?" shrieked Lyra, gripping a sandwich for dear life and racing to catch up with her friends.

"It's like a badger with a bad attitude!" shouted Banjo.

"Not just a bad attitude either, but sharp teeth and razor-sharp claws too."

"IF ANYONE IS STILL HOLDING A SANDWICH, THROW IT OVER YOUR SHOULDER!" shouted Mo.

"Bye bye, sandwich!" sighed Lyra, doing as Mo asked.

"WHICH WAY SHOULD WE RUN?"

asked Banjo, darting in three directions at once.

"FOLLOW ME!!!"

said Mo. **"And don't stop running till we get to Wyoming!"**

By the time the five friends reached the State of Wyoming they didn't just need a drink, a lie-down, something to eat, twenty minutes of total silence to get their breath back and a place to cool down fast. They badly needed something to stop their tummies rumbling too.

"Don't gurgle too loudly," said Banjo, lying on his back with his hands on his tummy. "More Rocky Mountain bears, wolves, fish eagles, mountain lions and wolverines might be in the area!"

"I'm not sure sandwiches were such a good idea," panted Lily.

"I think you might be right," nodded Mo. "The good news is that if our sandwiches are all gone, there is no reason for anything to chase us."

"The bad news is that we don't have anything to eat," groaned Vern.

"We could eat berries," said Banjo.

"If we knew which ones weren't poisonous," frowned Vern.

"We could try eating grass," said Lily.

"Yes, and we could try twitching our noses like rabbits too," sighed Lyra.

"Or mooing like cows," laughed Mo.

"I KNOW WHAT WE CAN EAT!" said Banjo, swinging his rucksack on to his lap and delving deep down to the very bottom. **"I'D FORGOTTEN ALL ABOUT THESE!"**

Lily, Lyra, Vern and Mo sat up excitedly and watched curiously as Banjo rummaged through his rucksack.

"CRISP, ANYBODY?!!!!"

he cheered, turning round triumphantly and raising his arm aloft. **"I packed a packet of crisps with my sandwiches too!"**

The faces of the other four friends lit up. OK, it wasn't a lovely freshly made, lovingly made, home-made sandwich, or the most nutritious snack in the world, but it wasn't a poisonous berry or a fistful of mountain grass either.

"FOUR CHEERS FOR BANJO!" shouted Vern, as good old, clever old Banjo held the crisp packet to his chest and prised it open with both hands.

"HIP HIP . . ."

"Why's the ground shaking?" whispered Lily, staring down at her trainers.

"Yes, why's the ground shaking?" frowned Lyra. **"It wasn't shaking before."**

The five friends sat motionless on the grass.

Pine cones were dropping like rain from the trees, and wild flowers were shedding petals around their ankles.

"You don't think it's an earthquake, do you?" whispered Lily.

"RUN!" hollered Mo, heading for cover. "BIGFOOT IS COMING!"

Lily looked at Lyra, Lyra looked at Banjo and Banjo looked at Vern.

"Who's Bigfoot?" they chorused.

"THAT'S BIGFOOT!" pointed Mo.

The four friends wheeled round and

gasped. A huge hairy ape man as tall as a giraffe and as hairy as a buffalo was loping across the meadow straight towards them!

"WHAT SORT OF CRISPS HAVE YOU JUST OPENED?" hollered Mo.

"MONSTER CRISPS!" shouted Banjo.

"MONSTER CRISPS!!!!????" gasped his four friends.

"HOW WAS I TO KNOW????!!!" flapped Banjo.

"LOOK AT THE SIZE OF HIS FEET!" gasped Vern.

"LOOK AT THE SIZE OF

HIS FOOTPRINTS!" shuddered Mo.

"WHAT IF HE TREADS ON US?" gasped Lily.

"WHAT IF HE SQUASHES US?" gasped Lyra.

"WHAT IF HE FLATTENS US INTO PANCAKES, TAKES US HOME AND EATS US WITH MAPLE SYRUP?!" gulped Banjo.

"Banjo, quick! Throw the crisps over your shoulder!" shouted Lily. "Before it's too late!"

Lily was right. There was no time to lose. Bigfoot was closing in fast, and he only had one thing on his mind.

"RUN

FOR

YOUR

LIVES!"

hollered Mo, sprinting hard and fast through the pine-cone-littered forest. "And don't stop running till we get to Colorado!"

By the time the five friends reached the State of Colorado they didn't just need a drink, a lie-down, something to eat, twenty minutes of total silence to get their breath back, a place to cool down fast and something to stop their tummies rumbling. They needed a new pair of trainers each too!

But there was no time. Because **the ground was shaking EVEN MORE NOW!**

"OH NO," said Mo.

"OH NO WHAT?" murmured Vern.

"IT'S BIGGER FOOT!!!"

gasped Mo, pointing to the end of the valley.

"Who's BIGGER FOOT?" gasped Vern.

"BIGFOOT'S MUM!" gulped Mo.

The mouths of the five friends dropped open as a foot the size of a lorry crunched into view. It had toes the size of armchairs and toenails the size of car windscreens.

BOOM! echoed the valley, with each and every thunderous stride.

CRACK! went a forest of redwood trees, splintering under Bigger Foot's tread.

"RUN!"

shouted Mo. "Everybody run as fast as you can, and don't stop till we get to New Mexico!"

By the time the five friends reached
the State of New Mexico they didn't just
need a drink, a lie-down, something to
eat, twenty minutes of total silence to get
their breath back, a place to cool down
fast, something to stop their tummies
rumbling and a new pair of trainers each.

They needed new sets of lungs too.

But the ground was still shaking. And
shaking and shaking and shaking!

"OH NO," said Mo.

"WHAT NOW?" said Vern.

**"IT'S EVEN BIGGER
FOOT!!!"** gasped Mo, pointing high
above the skyline of the mountain range to
the eyeline of a huge hairy forehead.

"Who's EVEN BIGGER FOOT?" trembled Lily.
"BIGFOOT'S DAD!" gulped Mo.

If the five friends had thought they were in trouble before, they were in even bigger trouble now. They had been chased along the entire length of the Rocky Mountain range across seven states, from Canadian British Columbia all the way down to American New Mexico.
And now Bigfoot, Bigger Foot and Even Bigger Foot were ALL hot on their trail!

"I don't get it," panted Lyra, doubling over and steadying herself on a tree trunk as another giant footstep shook the valley floor. "Why are we still being chased by giant hairy monsters? **We gave them the crisps back in Wyoming!"**

All eyes turned to Banjo as the mountainside reverberated once more.

Banjo's eyeballs rattled with the impact of all the stomping and then lowered rather sheepishly towards the floor.

"Didn't we, Banjo?" frowned Lily, gripping her ponytail as tightly as she could to try to stop it from shaking.

"Errr . . . not exactly,"

mumbled Banjo, putting his hand back into his rucksack and pulling out the packet of crisps.

Lily, Vern, Lyra and Mo stared in disbelief.

"YOU WERE SUPPOSED TO THROW THEM OVER YOUR SHOULDER!" squawked Vern.

"But I'm hungry," whined Banjo, diving for cover as the seismic shock of an even bigger footstep thundered through the valley.

"WE'RE ALL HUNGRY!!!!!!" cried Lyra, wobbling like jelly.

"BUT NONE OF US WANT TO BE EATEN!"

Banjo crouched low and then froze as the Rocky Mountain sunshine suddenly faded.

"OH DEAR," he gasped, as the sky-scraping hairiness of Papa Bigfoot loomed, loped and lumbered into full and open view.

Boulders dislodged and bounced down mountainsides, and snow caps cracked and slid from rocky peaks as stride by shuddering stride the family of humungous, hairy, hungry mountain monsters drew nearer and nearer and nearer . . .

"They can smell your crisps, Banjo!" gulped Lily.

"They can smell us too!!" trembled Vern.

Quick as a flash, Mo raced forward, snatched the crisps from Banjo's hand and scattered them over the valley floor.

"RUN!" he shouted, his voice almost hoarse.

"For the very last time, run and run and run and run and run. Don't stop running till we get home!"

By the time the five friends reached home they didn't just need a drink, a lie-down, something to eat, twenty minutes of total silence to get their breath back, a place to cool down fast, something to stop their tummies rumbling, a new pair of trainers each and new sets of lungs.

They badly needed the ground not to be shaking too.

They were in luck. Lily's ponytail had definitely stopped bouncing and Banjo's eyeballs had definitely stopped rattling. To the five weary friends' utter relief, the hairy, hungry, big-footed monsters were nowhere to be seen.

Even better, they were home just in time for dinner!

"That was fun!" said Lily, massaging the backs of her calves.

"That was immense!" said Lyra, allowing her tummy to rumble once more.

"Kind of," frowned Banjo, peering into his rucksack with a sigh.

"Where shall we run tomorrow?" asked Vern, touching his toes and then jogging for home.

"Anywhere but a sandwich shop," smiled Mo.

Look out for the next Go, Mo, Go adventure . . .

Coming soon!